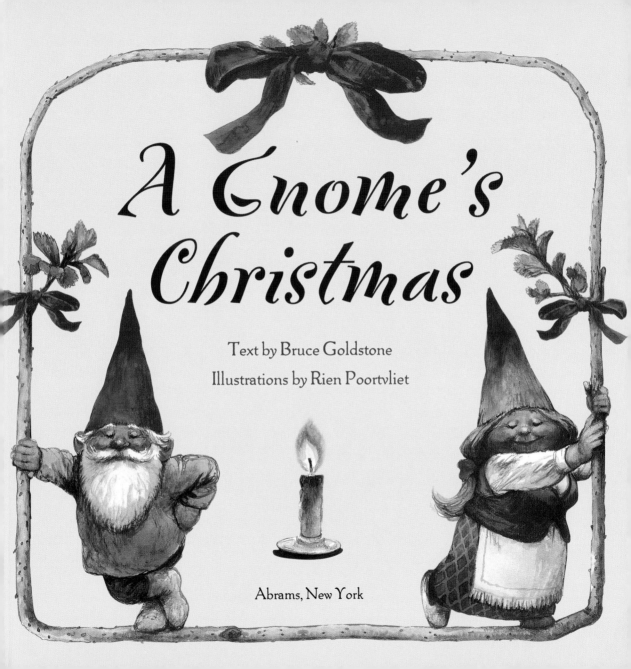

A Gnome's Christmas

Text by Bruce Goldstone

Illustrations by Rien Poortvliet

Abrams, New York

A Note About This Book

Not too long ago, a mysterious greenwood box was discovered in the rafters of a weathered barn in northern Finland. The finder, a no-nonsense mechanic who used the barn to repair snow machines, brought the box into the warmth of his home, where it was carefully inspected by his wife and young twin sons.

The small, perfectly square box smelled of fresh varnish. It had no visible hinges, latch, or keyhole, yet it was clearly hollow. When the father shook the box, he could hear something lightly shifting within. Yet he could find no opening.

After shaking the box and shaking it again, the mechanic and his wife lost interest and stashed it in a corner. Sometime the next day while the twins were playing, they remembered the box. Being twins, they were used to having the same thought at the same time.

The moment both twins' hands touched the box, it flipped open into two equal halves. The interior was lined in woven straw dyed ruby red. Atop each hollowed half lay neatly tied bundles of tiny paper sheets containing sheet music and writing in many languages, including Finnish, German, French, Dutch, Portuguese, Swedish, and Russian. These give a detailed description of a gnome's Christmas. No one knows how long the box was left in that Finnish barn or who put it there. Some experts, including the twin boys, suspect that the gnomes left it there on purpose. But if that is so, what was the reason?

The Month of Christmas

Gnomes know a lot. They know how to choose the tastier of two mushrooms. They know how to predict the weather by the feel of a mouse's fur or the scent of a falling leaf. They know how to talk a hungry fox out of stealing a hen's last egg. But perhaps the thing they know best is that Christmas lasts a month.

A gnome's Christmas extends from the arrival of Sinterklaas through the heartfelt and jocular exchanges of Edda Night. In every gnome home around the world, Christmas concludes one year and launches another. No gnome would miss it. Ever.

Sinterklaas Arrives (December 6)

Any gnome child will tell you that Sinterklaas and his assistant, Little Piet, leave their home in Spain each November. On his head, Sinterklaas wears a proud red miter, whose flame-shape recognizes the eternal Holy Spirit. The crosier in his hand, shaped like a shepherd's crook, symbolizes his divine authority. Little Piet carries an overstuffed sack, which doesn't symbolize anything, but does contain lots of goodies. He also wears a starchy, white, ruffled collar and a cap with a feather in it.

Together, Sinterklaas and Little Piet ride a huge white horse across the lands. Their long journey ends on December 6, when they visit each and every gnome brother and sister. Good little gnomes get treats from the sack. Bad little gnomes . . . well, there really are very few of those.

Of course, even young gnome children have a lot of questions about Sinterklaas. For instance, how can he visit every gnome in one night? The answer is simple—he has helpers. Nearly every gnome father from north to south has a red bishop's miter and carved wooden crosier stored away for that special night. He never hides this costume from his children. All he needs to do is explain that he is one of Sinterklaas's helpers. A neighborly mole, chipmunk, or shrew usually takes the role of Little Piet.

Gnome Gifts and the Mascot Hour

Gnomes love to give one another gifts, but they prefer to spread their giving out. In the month of Christmas, gifts begin to arrive with Sinterklaas, but they don't stop then. Hidden gifts pop up throughout the month. As gnomes are nocturnal, gnome children wake up each evening ready to face an exciting new night. Those nights are even more exciting during the Christmas month, when gnome children might wake up any evening to find a surprise that was tucked under their pillow during the day.

Every gnome gift is made by hand. The thought of buying something as a gift strikes gnomes as silly and a little cold. As gnomes say, "From the hands, from the heart." Of course, living four hundred years or more gives gnomes a lot of time to perfect their handicrafts.

Gifts of the Christmas season include wooly knitted mittens, hand-sewn puppets, and carved wooden toys of every description. Jointed horses and dolls ride in elegant carriages or trains. Family gifts might also include bowling games, toy chests, or a four-person toboggan.

The Mascot Hour comes sometime between the visit of Sinterklaas and Christmas Eve. It takes place whenever the family completes the year's mascot. Every gnome home has a mascot, a carved wooden figure hung over the mantel. Different animals bring different kinds of fortune. A deer mascot brings serenity; a bear brings strength. A parrot brings adventure; a snake brings security. Gnome families create a new mascot each year.

Everyone helps carry out this project. During the Mascot Hour, the old mascot is taken down and the new one hung in its place. Old mascots are usually burned for good luck. But gnomes don't really need more luck, so they sometimes give them to local beavers for chipping, or rats, who like to collect them. The family then gathers for one hour, reviewing the year past and sharing their hopes for next year.

Traditionally, a bowl of porridge and a glass of wine are left out for the new mascot. Also traditionally, children wake up the next night to find that the mascot has drunk the wine and left the porridge.

Christmas Rounds (December 25)

Because gnomes are nocturnal, Christmas celebrations begin at nightfall on December 25. This is the best-loved night of the year, because it is the time of Christmas Rounds.

On Christmas, the entire gnome family bundles up and goes out into the cold in search of animals who are having trouble getting through the winter. Before Christmas Rounds begin, families pack baskets of nuts, fruits, and cakes to give to hungry animals. Then the family—mother, father, and twins, for gnomes always have twins—trudges happily through the snow, singing carols and watching for signs of life.

All animals know the sweet sound of gnomes singing in winter could mean a tasty treat or a helping hand. One by one or two by two they come out of woods and warrens, nooks and nests. In fact, lots of animals look forward to Christmas Rounds almost as much as the gnomes do. Mice, weasels, and stoats are particularly fond of making paper lanterns that they carry on Christmas Night to signal to gnomes that they are welcome visitors.

Friends draw near.
Come out! Come here!
It's time for Christmas Rounds.
Food for all,
Both big and small
Together. Christmas Rounds!
Kindness and
A helping hand
Are yours on Christmas
Rounds.

Frogs have a particularly tough time getting through cold winters, so gnome families make sure to bring them nutritious stew during Christmas Rounds. Although frogs are notoriously self-centered, one or two in any pond will manage to croak out a rough thank-you. Of course, gnomes would feed them even without it. They don't expect to be thanked for any of the good deeds done during Christmas Rounds. They view their acts as happy duties which help to keep the world in balance.

Gnomes provide many kinds of assistance during Christmas Rounds. If a bird family is living in a nest they never quite got around to finishing, gnomes will gather to complete it. The walls of rabbit warrens sometimes fall during midwinter thaws. Gnomes are happy to help rebuild, though they must do so with care. The thumping hind legs of a hare excited to see his new home can deliver a painful kick.

In many regions, Christmas Rounds include paw and hoof inspections for running animals, such as deer, moose, or wolves. Gnomes remove any painful thorns or splinters and also rub in protective ointments and waxes made just for this ritual.

Christmas Rounds bring refreshment and joy on a cold winter's night, but then, gnomes are used to taking care of things. They help animals and tend plants every night of the year. On Christmas Night, they simply take time to celebrate their way of life. As one proverbial exchange puts it:

"Every night is Christmas Night when there's an animal in need." To which a gnome is certain to respond, "And there's always an animal in need."

Edda Night (January 6)

The month of Christmas ends on January 6 with Edda Night. For this community celebration, gnomes from a village gather together to share poems and songs that they have written for the occasion. These personal and humorous works often poke fun at the foibles of villagers or express amused bafflement at the ridiculous ways of mankind. The mood during the Edda Night can be raucous and the festival often goes until sunrise. The ceremony ends with everyone holding hands and whispering this New Year blessing:

May this year be full of proud deeds
and silly games, beautiful songs
and hearty feasts, clever jokes,
loving friends,
and enough surprises
to keep us on our toes.

Music and Merriment

The homes of gnomes ring with the sounds of song and play during Christmas. Despite their height, gnomes possess surprisingly rich voices. They are also highly vocal game players, likely to accompany any amusement with a gleeful whoop, chortle, or giggle.

Songs of the Season

Gnomes play many different instruments, including the recorder, flute, kazoo, guitar, banjo, and an elongated horn somewhere between a trumpet and a trombone. However, the songs of Christmas are most often accompanied by the delicately plucked strings of a zither or harp.

A zither is essentially a set of strings stretched over a box, which acts as a resonating chamber. Christmas carolers usually include at least one zither player (or zitherer, as gnomes like to say). Harps are a bit heavy to lug around from house to house.

However, in gnome homes, the sound of harp strings is considered an essential part of every Christmas. Most gnome harpists are women—in fact, gnomes associate harps with motherhood. "The harp takes care of the hearth."

Many gnome families begin and end each night with song. During the month of Christmas, gnome children might sing a different carol each evening before school. After dinner, the family holds an informal concert. As singing lightens the heart, it is also considered a helpful aid to digestion. Traditional lullabies soothe children to sleep with the dawn.

The Gathering Song

One of the most popular carols, "The Gathering Song," is also an opportunity for improvisation and verbal showing-off. Gnomes like to dare one another to come up with new lists of animals for each verse of the song. The translation given here offers just three of the countless possible variations.

Many other animals join gnomes in their Christmas caroling. Unfortunately, the most enthusiastic are the woodchucks. Utterly tone deaf, woodchucks nonetheless love to sing. Well, they call it singing, anyway. How many gnome wives have looked out the window with a sigh to utter that familiar holiday refrain—"Oh dear, it's the woodchucks"?

The Gathering Song

A Gnome's Lullaby

Bedtime rituals take place at sunrise. Every gnome is born with a twin. The young twins soon learn to help each other prepare for bed. It is a bittersweet moment for all gnome parents when their children first learn to perform the morning cap-tuck. Each twin gently tugs down the other twin's cap to cover the eyes and shield the sun's rays.

This traditional gnome lullaby is especially useful during Christmas, when excitement and anticipation can make it hard for young gnomes to fall asleep.

A Gnome's Lullaby

The Kissing Song

Even without mistletoe, gnome couples find plenty of opportunities for holiday kisses. All a gnome husband needs to do is hum the opening bars of "The Kissing Song." At the end of the song, a warm kiss is all but certain.

The Kissing Song

Gnome Games

Playful sports and sometimes rowdy pastimes are another key part of every gnome's Christmas season. Families play games both indoors and out, and are often joined by animals who have a little spare time on their hands.

Gnomes often train insect friends to perform remarkable stunts. Training sessions take place in secret so that these fantastic feats can be revealed during Christmas. On any morning during the month, a gnome father might return home and proudly announce an insect show before it is time to tuck into bed. He will then open the front door and invite the surprise guest inside.

Insect shows often begin with simple stunts, such as grasshoppers hopping through hoops or a line of ants forming a crisp, five-pointed star. More complicated displays follow, such as spiders spinning webs in the shape of snowflakes or bees buzzing a Christmas carol in perfect unison.

All gnomes, children and adults, love to play pranks. As one saying goes, "A napping gnome is fair game." Twins might take turns tossing rings onto their sleeping father's cap, replace his honey tea with vinegar, or tie a pie plate to his beard.

Even a cranky gnome will forgive the most outlandish tomfoolery during the festive times of Christmas month.

Cap-Tap-Tap

Another holiday pastime is Cap-Tap-Tap. To play, a gnome places miniature red caps on the fingers of one hand. He hides a ball of wax under one cap. Children then take turns plucking off hats. The child who finds the wax gets to light the candles in the Christmas center-piece and pick a favorite story. The parent then creates a shadow-puppet play telling the story, using the miniature caps to create gnome shadows.

Hip-Hop-Hup

The game of Hip-Hop-Hup is a favorite of gnomes and their neighbors. Essentially a game of follow-the-leader, in Hip-Hop-Hup followers try to do exactly what the leader does, be it hopping, singing, eating, or yodeling. When a duck is the leader, he might quack and flap four and a half times. All other players try to repeat the action. The duck decides who produced the best copy and names that player leader for the next round. Playing Hip-Hop-Hup with snakes poses special challenges, both for the snakes and for other players. The same goes for spiders and centipedes.

Outdoor games of the Christmas season include sledding, skating, skiing, making snowmen, and having snowball-tossing contests. While some sleds are carefully constructed, young gnomes also delight in old-fashioned nutshell sleds and dried-leaf toboggans.

Holiday Treats

Gnome holiday tables buckle under fruit cobblers, fresh-baked breads, honey biscuits, and more. Their vegetarian diet allows gnomes to share their favorite treats with all birds and beasts. The traditional Christmas dinner begins with rich mushroom broth, followed by potato stew served with cheesy rolls.

The One-Der is a Christmas specialty. Like many gnome traditions, it allows for improvisation and a creative touch. Here's a typical One-Der recipe:

1 walnut
1 acorn
1 almond
1 fig
1 date

The fruit is first soaked in grog, mead, or other lightly alcoholic beverage. The nuts and drunken fruits are then combined together, using a grinder or mortar and pestle. The paste is formed into balls and rolled in cocoa or chopped nuts.

Gnome cooks delight in varying the recipe. Indeed, the recipe never turns out the same way twice, due to variations in the sizes of each nut or fruit. That's why gnomes say "No two One-Ders are alike."

Traditional Horseshoe Cookies are often baked on January 7 to give gnome children something to look forward to after Sinterklaas has gone. The horseshoe shape represents the hoofprints left by Sinterklaas's horse as he rides away.

Of course, many of the treats that gnomes bake are shared with animals during Christmas Rounds. Over the years, gnomes have learned how to make holiday treats that will delight anybody, from a shrew to a tiger. Mice adore a cheese casserole, but squirrels prefer a nutmeat pudding. Foxes will sit up and wag for a taste of garlic pie. Tug Bread is a thick and chewy bread baked in a metal ring. It is so adored by beavers that most everyone nowadays just calls it Beaver Bread.

Tales of the Season

Gnomes love to tell tales and share poems at all times of the year. Here are just a few of their Christmas favorites.

Sinterklaas's Helpers

The tradition of dressing up as Sinterklaas and Little Piet to help them deliver their goodies is commemorated in this oft-repeated Christmas poem.

Cut the cloth to make the miter.
Put the final stitches in.
Tie it on a little tighter.
Everybody pitches in
   to help Sinterklaas.

Make a soft and baggy bonnet
With a feather in the back.
Collar starched with ruffles on it
And a big gray cotton sack
   to help Little Piet.

We can make their job go faster
If we help them bringing toys.
So we dress up as the pastor
And go forward singing joys
 to help Sinterklaas.

Make sure that your back is stronger
If you choose the cotton bag.
Each step makes your journey longer
When your back begins to sag
 to help Little Piet.

Even in the chilly weather
Whether snow or wind that's freezing.
We can do the work together
Warmed up by the hearts we're pleasing
 to help Sinterklaas.

The Christmas Wish

A field mouse, a finch, and a gnome were skating on a frozen pond one Christmas evening. From the firm safety of the pond's bank, an unhappy pig watched their graceful spins and leaps.

"I wish I could skate on the pond," moaned the pig. "I would make a great skater."

"Well, tell us before you get on the ice," tittered the field mouse.

"Yes," chirped the finch. "We don't want to drown when umpteen hundred pounds of pig crash through the ice."

The gnome would normally have laughed at this good-natured ribbing, but since it was Christmas, he decided to grant the pig's wish instead.

"Go ahead and give it a try," said the gnome.

The pig's ears perked right up and he slid cautiously onto the pond. Not a crack or groan came from the ice. The pig started to slide and skate in elegant circles and eights.

"You see," oinked the delighted pig, "I can skate. Why, I'm a much much better skater than any of you."

And with that the pig launched into a huge leap, turning in the air and landing on the ice with a loud CRACK.

The shivering pig looked quite sheepish as it climbed out of the pond and returned to the bank to watch the skaters.

Moral: Christmas miracles will lift you up, but gloating pigs are quickly drenched.

Pollitt's Wonder

Pollitt began to wonder when he saw a full moon early one December. Taking his nightly tour of the local fields, he noticed that the soft moonlight hung in the air like a heavy curtain put up to prevent a draft. Pollitt had always been a straightforward and self-assured gnome. Yet something about the dim moonlight triggered a strange uncertainty in him.

"I wonder if the moon is happy," wondered Pollitt.

Of course, this was a very difficult question to answer. He pondered for a while longer, and then headed home with a muddled head.

"Is something wrong?" asked his wife Sonje as soon as he walked in the door, for she had never seen such a look of profound puzzlement on his face.

Pollitt explained his wonder.

"Yes," agreed Sonje, "That is a hard one. But I think that the moon must be happy, because she shines so brightly for us."

"That is what I was afraid of," replied Pollitt. "For the moon's light comes and goes. If moonlight means it is happy, then the moon is moody at best."

Pollitt started to feel sad, which is an uncomfortable feeling for a gnome.

The next night, Pollitt returned to his rounds but was again struck by wonder when the moon emerged from behind a cloud. A passing bat noticed the frozen gnome staring up and decided to stop for a chat. Bats are much more friendly than most people think.

When Pollitt explained his quandary, the bat flapped up into the air. Bats do their best thinking in the air.

"Well," said the bat, "I suppose the moon is neither happy nor unhappy. It is merely a reflection and has no true feelings of its own."

"Possibly true," said Pollitt, "but you are blind to the moon's beautiful light. If you could see it, you would sense that the moon must be happy at least some of the time."

Each night, Pollitt would go about his chores and errands, and each night he would look up to see the waning moon grow darker and darker. Pollitt grew sadder and sadder. Going out each night became more and more difficult.

On the night of the new moon, Pollitt went outside with a tear already beginning in the corner of his eye. He knew that he wouldn't be able to see the moon. He thought, therefore, that the moon must be terribly unhappy.

Sitting on a small hillock, Pollitt looked up into the sky and began to cry.

An owl heard the soft blubbing. Gnomes never cry, so the curious owl simply had to fly down and find out the cause of this oddity.

"Our friend the moon is so unhappy that she cannot shine at all," cried Pollitt.

"Nonsense," hooted the owl. "On tonight of all nights you should know better."

"Why tonight?" asked Pollitt.

"It is Christmas Night, when gnomes celebrate generosity and caring."

Pollitt gasped—he had been so absorbed in his wonder that he had forgotten all about the most important holiday of the year.

"The moon is not unhappy," continued the owl. "She is merely being generous. For the moon is the most generous of all of us. She is giving the stars a chance to shine. She knows that they would feel jealous if she were always the brightest thing in the sky."

Pollitt saw the sense in this and began to feel better about the moon.

"Here comes your family on Christmas Rounds," said the owl, nudging Pollitt up. "Join them and stop worrying about the moon. She does not worry about you."

Pollitt waved at the owl as it flew away and then ran to join his family on their Christmas visits. He hurried along with a newfound excitement. He wanted to be as generous as the moon.

*P*ollitt's tale, like so many gnome Christmas stories, regenerates the spirit. With their faith and energy restored, gnomes go forth into a merry new year. Still, they leave the season behind with a pinch of reluctance, as suggested by one lasting memento. The holiday centerpiece, usually a simple candle surrounded by dried greenery or pine cones, stays on the family dining table throughout the year. A gnome's home would look empty without it.

Designed by Celina Carvalho

Production Manager: Jonathan Lopes

Library of Congress Cataloging-in-Publication Data
Goldstone, Bruce.
A gnome's Christmas / by Bruce Goldstone ; illustrated by Rien Poortvliet.
p. cm.
Summary: A mysterious box found in an old barn in Finland contains papers which detail
how gnomes celebrate Christmas with games, music, food, and stories.
ISBN 978-0-8109-5017-7
[1. Gnomes—Fiction. 2. Christmas—Fiction.] I. Poortvliet, Rien, ill. II. Title.
PZ7.G579Gn 2004
[Fic]—dc22
2004003055

Printed and bound in China
10 9 8 7 6 5

Abrams Books are available at special discounts when purchased in quantity for premiums and promotions
as well as fundraising or educational use. Special editions can also be created to specification. For details, contact
specialmarkets@abramsbooks.com or the address below.

THE ART OF BOOKS SINCE 1949
115 West 18th Street
New York, NY 10011
www.abramsbooks.com